The Ugly Old Scarecrow

...and other stories

Enid Blyton

The Ugly Old Scarecrow

...and other stories

Bounty Books

Published in 2015 by Bounty Books,
a division of Octopus Publishing Group Ltd,
Carmelite House,
50 Victoria Embankment,
London EC4Y 0DZ
www.octopusbooks.co.uk

An Hachette UK Company
www.hachette.co.uk
Enid Blyton ® Text copyright © 2015 Hodder & Stoughton Ltd.
Illustrations copyright © 2015 Octopus Publishing Group Ltd.
Layout copyright © 2015 Octopus Publishing Group Ltd.

Illustrated by Jane Etteridge.

ISBN: 978-0-75372-942-7

A CIP catalogue record for this book is available from the British Library.

CONTENTS

The Very Old Kettle

There was once a fine kettle belonging to old Mother Mimble. It sat on her stove all day long and sang. It bubbled with joy, and sang very loudly indeed when there was a good hot fire and the water inside it boiled.

Mother Mimble had had her kettle for years and years. When she was young and strong she had bought it bright and new. She had polished it well, and every day it had shone like silver. It had boiled water for thousands of cups of tea, and had filled the old brown teapot hundreds of times. It was a very happy kettle.

It knew all Mother Mimble's children. There was Dinah, the eldest; Judy and Punch, the twins; Bobby-

Boy, Sally and the baby. They all knew the kettle too, and loved to see it sitting on the hob, telling them it was nearly tea-time.

Then one day, when Mother Mimble's children were all grown up, and nobody lived in the little cottage

except the old woman herself, a sad thing happened to the old kettle.

A hole appeared at the bottom of it! Mother Mimble poured the water in, and as fast as it went in at the top, it came out at the bottom. It was no good as a kettle any longer.

'Ah, well,' said Mother Mimble, taking it up and having a good look at it. 'You've lasted a long time, old kettle. Now I must buy a new one, and you must be thrown away.'

She took it down the garden and threw it over the hedge, for she was an untidy old woman. The kettle fell into

the middle of a blackberry bush and slipped through the thorns. It came to rest on the sandy earth and stood there, wondering greatly, for it had never been out of the kitchen before. It missed the boiling, bubbling water, and could not think what had happened. Where was the bright fire, the shining poker, the twinkling fender?

The old kettle stayed under the blackberry bush for a long time. No one saw it; no one came and called out 'Now then, kettle, boil up for tea!' It was quite alone, and very homesick for the hob where it had stood for so many years. Everyone had loved it, and now it was nothing to anyone. The old kettle was very sad.

Then one day in spring, when the sun came slipping through the bramble-bush, a perky robin came hopping near. By him was his little mate. He suddenly saw the old kettle, and flew to it with a delighted squeak.

'Here is a fine thing!' he called in a trilling voice. 'See, wife – an old kettle that has stood in the home of men.'

'Oh, I should *love* to have my nest in something belonging to humans!' said his little mate. 'They are our friends, and it would be nice to bring our little ones up in something that has belonged to them.'

'I was brought up in a saucepan myself!' said the cock robin, puffing out his chest.

'And I lived in an old watering-can,' said his wife. 'We *couldn't* find anything better than this, dear. Let's start making our nest at once.'

The cock robin perched on the handle of the kettle and peeped inside. In a moment he hopped right down into the kettle itself, and explored it thoroughly.

'Plenty of room, plenty of room!' he called to his wife. 'Come and look.'

Before very long the two robins were hard at work building the prettiest little nest you ever saw. They found some hay and plenty of dead leaves. They dug up some moss, and brought that, too, in their beaks. They tucked it here and there, and soon the kettle held a warm and cosy nest inside.

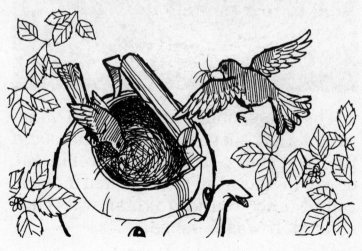

Then the robins lined it with some
rabbit fluff they had found and some
fine dog hairs. The mother robin sat
down in the nest and worked herself
round and round to make it cup-
shaped. It was finished!

'I am sure no other bird in the whole of the kingdom has such a fine home as this lovely old kettle,' said the mother robin proudly.

'It's so cosy and comfortable,' said the cock robin. 'I *love* this old kettle.'

How pleased and proud the kettle was! How it longed to bubble and sing as it used to do! It was very happy indeed, and loved to feel the little feet of the two robins perching on its handle.

Then came the pretty eggs. There were four of them, speckled brown, and they lay cosily in the nest all together. The mother robin sat on them all day long, whilst her husband sang sweetly to her, or went to find tasty grubs and caterpillars. The kettle thought it had really never been so happy before. This

was much better than sitting on a hob!

One by one the little eggs cracked, and the funniest babies came out. The mother robin was so pleased with them! She and the father took turns at finding food for the hungry little things. The kettle thought that their wide-open yellow beaks were simply lovely. It longed to be a robin and go to find something to put into them.

It was a sad day for the kettle when the baby robins learnt to fly, and went away with their mother and father.

'Goodbye, old kettle,' said the cock robin, perching on the handle for the last time. 'We have loved living inside you. Goodbye!'

Once more the kettle settled down to lonely days. Then one morning a little girl and boy came by. They parted the brambles and peeped at the kettle.

The Very Old Kettle

'Oh, look, James!' said the little girl. 'There's an old kettle here with the loveliest nest inside! Let's take it to show Mother. Perhaps she will let us keep it in our museum.'

The two children picked up the old kettle and took it home. Their mother was delighted to see the lovely nest so carefully made inside.

'Yes, you must certainly put this in your museum,' she said to the children. 'All your school friends will be pleased to see it when they come to tea.'

So the old kettle was put into the little museum that the children had in their playroom. They had shells there, and dried seaweed, curious stones, a shark's tooth and an old arrow-head. They put the kettle right in the very middle.

'There!' said the little girl. 'Doesn't that look fine! It's the very best thing we've got, isn't it, James?'

'Yes,' said James, patting the kettle. 'Somebody must have thrown it away because it was old and broken, but now it will be happy again because we want it. What fun to show the little nest inside it to all our friends!'

So once again the old kettle was happy and proud, and longed to sing. It is still in the playroom, and if ever you go to tea with them you will see it when they show you the lovely little nest inside.

Louise and Bobs have an Adventure

One very sunny morning Louise's mother said that Bobs could go with Louise for a little walk in the fields. So Louise whistled for Bobs – she was quite good at whistling – and the two of them set off down the lane.

When they had gone a little way they came to a little white gate that led across the fields. So Louise climbed over it, and Bobs squeezed under it, and there they were in the grass that was thick with daisies and buttercups!

Louise sang loudly and Bobs barked madly. It was such a lovely morning that they both felt they really must make a noise. They ran races – but Bobs always won, no matter how fast Louise went. Louise picked a bunch of

Louise and Bobs have an Adventure

daisies to take home to Katie, her little sister. Bobs found an old rat-hole and began to dig so hard that the earth and grass flew up in the air all over Louise!

'Don't, Bobs!' she cried. But Bobs went on and on, so Louise ran away from him and hid behind a bush. Bobs was good at playing hide-and-seek. Louise watched him digging and digging, and then at last he got tired of it. He put his nose up and looked round for Louise.

'Wuff!' he said.

Louise didn't say a word. She just crouched down behind the bush so that not even the top of her golden head showed.

Bobs cocked both his ears up and stared all round in surprise. Where in the world could Louise have disappeared to? It was most mysterious!

'Wuff, wuff, WUFF!' he barked, which meant, 'Come along, Louise, and show me where you are.'

But Louise didn't move, though she

badly wanted to laugh. Bobs had such
sharp ears she knew that he would
hear even the smallest giggle. Then
Bobs put his nose to the ground to
smell where Louise's feet had been

and he ran round and round a few
times, sniffing hard. At last he found
where Louise's shoes had walked, and
he followed the smell of them with his
nose.

He went across the grass – he went
through a clump of buttercups – he
came to Louise's bush – and then, with
a loud bark he threw himself on her
and the two of them rolled over and
over and over!

'I've found you!' barked Bobs.

'Yes, you have,' said Louise. 'Now it's your turn to hide!'

But Bobs had just caught sight of something that put hide-and-seek quite out of his head! He had seen a rabbit bobbing up and down by the stream! A rabbit!

'Wuff!' cried Bobs, in delight, and he shot after the rabbit. He went so fast that Louise couldn't possibly catch him up. She was quite cross with him.

'Bobs! Don't play with rabbits now! Play with *me!*' she cried. But Bobs didn't come back.

'I shall go on without you, Bobs!' called Louise, and she climbed over the stile that led into the next field. Still Bobs didn't come. So Louise went on by herself. The buttercups were like a carpet of gold everywhere. The bees hummed, and on the hawthorn hedges the white may lay like dazzling snow. It smelt very sweet, too. Louise forgot about Bobs as she danced through the buttercup field.

She went down a little path that led to the river, and came back home another way. Her mother was picking flowers in the garden.

'Hello, dear!' she said, 'where's Bobs?'

'Oh, hasn't he come home?' said Louise, in alarm. 'Oh, Mummy! He went after a rabbit and wouldn't come with me – so I left him, thinking he would come home by himself.'

'Well, he hasn't,' said Mother. 'Never mind, I expect he's halfway down a rabbit-hole by now. He'll come back home when he's tired of being laughed at by rabbits he can't reach.'

But Bobs didn't come home. Louise called and whistled, and she and Mother went to the gate a dozen times to look for him, but there was no sign of him at all.

'Naughty little dog!' said Mother. 'Sandy! Sandy! Come here. You must come with us and look for Bobs.'

Sandy was the other dog that lived at the farm. He had a sandy head and a very good nose for smelling. He came running up.

'We've lost Bobs,' said Louise. 'You must help us to find him, Sandy.'

'Wuff, wuff!' said Sandy, wagging his tail fast. He ran down the lane with Mother and Louise. They came to the white gate. Louise climbed over it, Sandy squeezed under it, but Mother opened it and went through it. Sandy ran all over the field with his nose to the ground.

Suddenly, Mother, Louise and Sandy lifted their heads and listened.

'I can hear Bobs barking!' said Louise, in great astonishment.

Louise and Bobs have an Adventure

'Yes, but it's such a funny bark!' said her Mother. 'It sounds so far away – sort of muffled – as if he were underground or something.'

'Oh, Mummy, do you think he's managed to get right down a rabbit-hole and can't get back again?' cried Louise, with tears in her eyes.

'Of course not,' said her Mother. 'He is much too big to get down a rabbit-hole. Listen!'

So they all listened again – and then Sandy set off at a great pace to the stream-side. He came to a tree, and began to scrape his paws against it, barking all the time!

Louise and her Mother hurried over to the tree too. It was an old, old willow tree – and inside it, deep down, they could hear poor Bobs barking!

'Look,' said Mother, pointing to the tree-trunk, 'Bobs went up the tree – and down through this crack – and fell into the hollow below and couldn't get out! I expect a rabbit went that way and he thought he could too!'

'Oh, Mummy, we were playing hide-and-seek, and Bobs meant to hide from me,' said Louise. 'Oh, I do think he's clever to choose such a good place! Bobs! Bobs! we're going to rescue you!'

'Woof, wooof, woooof!' said Bobs, scrabbling about in the tree below. 'Woof!'

'How can we rescue him?' said Mother. 'He is so far down – and the hole is so small!'

But Sandy knew how to rescue Bobs! He began to scrape away at the old, old willow tree, and the trunk flew to pieces! It was no stronger than cork!

Louise and Bobs have an Adventure

Louise broke pieces off too, and soon there was a big enough hole to look right in and see Bobs away down where the roots of the tree were!

'Woof!' said Bobs, looking up, his two eyes shining like lanterns in the darkness of the tree.

'Woof!' said Louise. 'Silly dog! Getting yourself lost in a hollow tree! Come now – jump! The hole is big enough for me to catch you as you jump.'

Bobs jumped – and Mother and Louise caught him and pulled him out.

'Wuff, wuff, woof, woof!' said Bobs, licking Louise and her Mother in delight, and then tearing off round the field like a mad thing to stretch his legs.

'Well, that *was* an adventure!' said Mother, as they all went home again. 'Bobs! Next time you play hide-and-seek, just choose an easier place to get out of!'

'Woof!' said Bobs, which meant 'Certainly, mistress!'

The Apple That Couldn't Be Found

Trip was being tiresome. He was a pixie, and when he was tiresome, his mother didn't know what to do with him. He upset this, and broke that, spilt something else, and tore his clothes in a dozen places.

'Oh, for goodness' sake, Trip!' said Dame Tuppy at last. 'Anyone would think you were under a spell! Do you want me to wallop you with the yard-broom?'

'Oh no, Ma!' said Trip Tuppy the pixie. 'Don't do that.'

'Well, you just sit quiet for a bit,' said Dame Tuppy. 'You've broken a glass, spilt the milk, upset the sugar, and torn your jacket. That's quite enough for one morning.'

The Apple That Couldn't Be Found

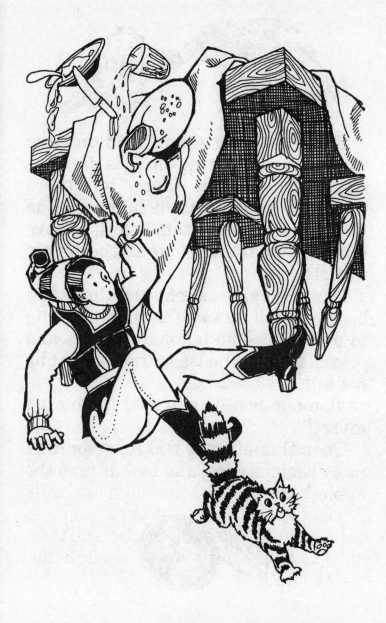

Trip sat down – but he didn't see what he was sitting on. He *thought* there was a chair there, but there wasn't. So he sat down bump on the floor, caught at the table-cloth to save himself – and down came all the dinner things!

Dame Tuppy caught up the yard-broom, and Trip saw that he was going to feel it – so he burst into tears and pretended that he was terribly hurt by his fall.

'Boo-hoo-hoo!' he wept. 'I've hurt myself.'

Then Dame Tuppy was sorry for him. She dried his eyes, and took him to the apple-barrel.

'Here is a nice red apple for you,' she said. 'Take it out on the hill and eat it, Trip. Be a good pixie, and run off for a while.'

So Trip took the apple and ran off. He went to the top of the hill near by and sat down. He could see such a lot of things from there. Cows and sheep, horses and goats, dogs, rabbits, hens and ducks. It was very hot, and Trip yawned.

I'll lie down for a minute before I eat my apple, he thought. So he lay down – and soon he was fast asleep.

When he woke up, he looked for his apple, for he was hungry. But it wasn't on the ground beside him! It had gone.

'It must have rolled down the hill!' said Trip, very much upset. 'I must go and look for it.'

He went down the hill, looking carefully in every corner. Before long he came to Blue-shoes' cottage. Blue-shoes was in the garden, hanging out some clothes. She was munching something, and Trip felt certain it was his apple.

'Hi!' he called indignantly. 'You're eating my apple that rolled into your garden.'

Blue-shoes was very cross. She took a stick and ran after him.

'I'm eating a cake I made myself!' she cried. 'You naughty little pixie, saying I was eating your apple. Why, I wouldn't do such a thing!'

Trip got one whack, and then escaped. He went on down the hill, searching everywhere. Soon he came to Flip's hut. Flip was a surly gnome. He sat at the door of the hut, eating something red. Trip ran up to him.

'Give me my apple!' he cried. 'That's mine! It rolled down the hill!'

Flip got up and caught hold of the pixie. He shook him well, and then sat him down suddenly.

'Don't you know a tomato when you see one?' he asked. 'Do you suppose I'd eat an apple belonging to you?'

Trip crept away with tears in his eyes. It certainly was a tomato that Flip was eating.

He hunted again, but no sign of his apple could he find. At last, right at the bottom of the hill, he came to the village postman's house. The postman was sitting in the garden, drinking lemonade with his mother, for it was a very hot afternoon. Under the table lay something red and round.

'My apple!' cried Trip. He ran into the garden without even an "Excuse me", dived under the table, and caught at the red thing. The postman was so surprised that his lemonade went down the wrong way, and he began to choke.

'Who is this rude little pixie?' asked the postman's mother in a cold sort of voice.

'He's stealing the new red ball I bought for my dog!' the postman cried suddenly as Trip went off towards the gate again.

He ran after the pixie and caught him. Sure enough Trip had got a fine red ball – not an apple as he had thought.

'I'm s-s-sorry!' said Trip. But it wasn't any use. He got a good shaking and one hard slap. Then he went off howling to his mother.

She heard all his story, but she didn't say much.

'You want to learn manners,' was all she said.

'Well, *some*body's got my apple,' said Trip sulkily. 'And if I find out who it is, I'll smack him hard – yes, I will!'

He stuck his hands into his pockets – then he took one out again – and in it was his own red apple!

'Oh!' said Trip, going very red. 'I remember now – I put it in my pocket before I went to sleep.'

'So it didn't roll down the hill after all,' said his mother. 'And look how bruised and battered it is now – it isn't worth eating. Well, you shouldn't have been so foolish. And, Trip, are you going to smack yourself hard? You said you were going to smack whoever had got your apple, you know!'

But Trip didn't answer. He ran away feeling very ashamed of himself, and gave the apple to Grunts, the pig. I haven't heard whether he has been a better pixie since – but I should think he has, wouldn't you?

Well Really, Old Grandad

One day Alice and Laura went to ask Mrs Straws, the farmer's wife, for twelve new-laid eggs.

'You can each take a basket,' said their mother, 'and bring back six, and that will be twelve altogether. Don't run when you bring the eggs back, in case you fall over and break them.'

Off went the two girls, swinging a little basket each. They liked going to the farm. They liked all the clucking hens, the quacking ducks, and the little skippetty lambs with their big woolly mothers.

They came to the farm and knocked at the door. Mrs Straws opened it. 'Good morning, my dears,' she said, 'I suppose you've come for the eggs. Well, now, step

Well Really, Old Grandad

inside a minute and I'll go and get them for you.'

They went into the big kitchen. It always smelt so nice. Alice sniffed. 'It smells of all the nice cakes you've ever baked, and of apple puddings and sausage rolls!' she said. 'I do like your kitchen.'

Mrs Straws laughed. 'I'm going to the hen-house for the eggs,' she said. 'Old Grandad is in the next room. If he calls for anything, go and see what he wants, will you?'

'Yes, Mrs Straws,' said Alice, hoping that Old Grandad *wouldn't* call.

Mrs Straws went out and no sooner had she closed the door behind her, than there came a shout from the next room.

'Annie! Annie, I want you!'

'He's calling Mrs Straws,' said Alice. 'Oh dear, he sounds a bit cross.'

'We'll have to go and see what he wants,' said Laura, and the two of them went into the next room. A big, red-faced man sat in an enormous armchair. He had whiskers all round his chin, and very bright blue eyes.

'Hello, who are you?' he said. 'Where's my granddaughter, Annie?'

'Gone to get some new-laid eggs, sir,' said Laura politely. 'Can we get you something? Mrs Straws said we were to see what you wanted, if you shouted.'

'Well, I want you to get my spectacles for me,' said Old Grandad. 'I had them on my knee a minute ago and now I can't find them anywhere! Bless my soul, I don't know where things go to! I lost my pencil yesterday, and my knife last week, and. . .'

'Goodness! Wherever do you put them?' said Alice.

'Nowhere! I've got a bad leg and I can't get out of this chair,' said Old Grandad. 'But Annie, she hunts all round the room for the things I lose and never finds them! It's a mystery, that's what it is. But you hurry up and find my glasses. They'll be round my chair somewhere.'

The children looked, but they couldn't see any glasses anywhere. Old Grandad got rather cross.

'Children nowadays don't seem able to

use their eyes!' he said. 'If only I could get out of this chair I'd find those glasses in a flash! Feel under the carpet, girl– they must be somewhere!'

But they weren't. The children stood up, looking hot and untidy for they had

been all over floor! Old Grandad was quite disgusted with them.

'You wait till Annie comes back!' he said. 'She'll see them. You don't know where to look.'

Alice stared at him. She had looked very hard indeed! It wasn't fair to say things like that. She pulled at the rug on Old Grandad's knees.

'Perhaps they're caught in the rug!' she said. 'Or maybe you're sitting on your glasses!'

'Now, now, don't you suppose I've shaken out the rug and felt the seat of the chair?' said Old Grandad.

Then Laura remembered something. At home there was an old chair like this one and once when she and Alice had sat in it, they had slid their hands down the sides of it and dear me, the things they had found there!

Perhaps Old Grandad's glasses had slipped down into the sides of *his* chair! Laura slid her hand down the right-hand side and her fingers felt something at once! She pulled out her hand and found that she was holding a pencil!

'Here's your pencil, anyway!' she said, and Old Grandad took it in delight. Then Alice put her hand down and brought up a big white hanky, neatly folded.

'So *that's* where my clean hanky went to!' said Old Grandad. 'Whatever next!'

Well, you really wouldn't believe the things the children found down the sides of Old Grandad's chair! There were two playing-cards, a fine penknife, a small book, a pipe, a pair of scissors, a stamp, a pound coin, a bag of sweets and the lost glasses as well!

Old Grandad kept shouting in surprise each time the children brought out something. Then he began to laugh and when Mrs Straws came back with the eggs, they were all three roaring with laughter. It was really funny to think of Old Grandad solemnly sitting in a chair where he had lost so many things!

'Oh!' said Mrs Straws, when she saw all the different things. 'Wherever did they come from? You naughty Old Grandad, you don't mean to say you

Well Really, Old Grandad

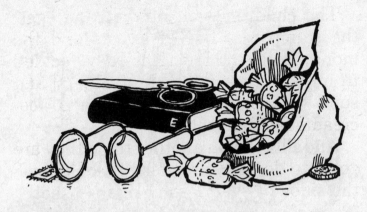

stuffed them down the sides of your chair?'

'No, Annie, no, they must have slipped down,' said Old Grandad, chuckling. 'Here are your scissors and your little book. And here you are, girls, a bag of sweets, a stamp and two pound coins, they're yours!'

'Oh no, *we* didn't put them down there,' said Alice.

'No, but you pulled them out, and you deserve them for being so clever!' said Old Grandad. 'You buy something nice, and next time you come for eggs you can feel down the sides of my old chair again!'

The children went off with the eggs, the stamp, the bag of sweets and the money. They did feel rich! They decided to buy Mummy a bunch of violets, and some chocolate for Daddy, and ice-creams for themselves.

And I'll tell you another thing they are going to do, they are going to look down the sides of every armchair they see!

Polly Piglet

Once upon a time there was a little piglet who lived all by herself in a big sty.

Her name was Polly Piglet, and she was round and fat and pink. She had a very funny nose that was useful for rooting about in the sty, and she had a very curly tail.

But Polly Piglet was very lonely. She peeped through the bars of her gate and saw the hens and the ducks, the lambs and the calves, and she wanted to play with them.

'I shall squeeze under this gate and go to play with those darling chicks,' said Polly Piglet. 'I don't like living by myself. Perhaps the hen will give me one of her chicks for my own.'

So she squeezed under the gate of her sty. It was a very tight squeeze because Polly was really very fat and very round. She panted and puffed and wriggled, but at last she managed to get through!

Polly Piglet scampered over to the brown mother-hen and her ten yellow chicks. 'Let me play with you!' she said. 'Give me one of your chicks for my own!'

But the yellow chicks were afraid of Polly Piglet, and they ran away, cheeping.

'Go away, you ugly piglet!' said the mother-hen, and she pecked poor Polly's nose.

Polly Piglet was sad. She saw the big white mother-duck nearby, and ran over to her. The duck had eight beautiful yellow ducklings.

'Let me play with you, please let me play with you!' cried Polly Piglet.

But the little ducklings were afraid, and they jumped into the pond with a splash.

'I don't like you, ugly piglet!' quacked the big duck, and splashed Polly with water.

Splish-splash went the big drops of water all over Polly Piglet. Some fell on her nose, some fell on her back, and some fell on her curly little tail. She didn't like it at all.

Poor Polly Piglet! She felt very sad and lonely. She walked on, and soon she saw four frisky lambs. Two had black noses, and they all had tails that wriggled and shook.

'Oh, what darlings!' cried Polly. 'How I would like one for a friend!'

She ran up to them. 'Please, little lambs, play with me,' she said. 'Do play with me. I know so many good games, and we could have fun together!'

But the lambs looked at Polly in fright. 'What is this ugly pink animal?' they bleated to one another. 'It frightens us. Let us run away!'

So they all ran away on their long legs, and their tails shook and wriggled as they went. They stood in a corner of the field and would not go near Polly Piglet.

She was very upset. Her tail lost its pretty curl and hung down straight.

'Nobody wants to be friends with me,' she said sadly. 'I am alone and by myself, and I don't like it a bit.'

Polly Piglet went on her way, looking for somebody else to talk to. Soon she saw two dear little red-and-white animals, with big brown eyes.

'They are baby cows!' said Polly to herself. 'Little calves! How sweet they look! I am sure they would love to be friends with a little pig like me.'

So she ran up to the little calves, and spoke to them in her piggy voice. 'I am very lonely,' she said. 'I have no one to play with. Please be friends with me. Won't you come and live in my sty? It is big enough for all of us!'

The little calves looked at Polly out of their soft brown eyes. One of them

swung his tail round him to swish off a fly.

'What! Live with a queer-looking piglet like you!' said the calves. 'No thank you!' And they stamped in a big brown puddle, and splashed a lot of mud all over poor Polly Piglet.

'Now you are a funny spotted pig!' they said.

Polly Piglet ran on, and then she came to where some children were playing games together. There was a baby in a pram, wearing a big bonnet. She looked very sweet.

'Oh, if only she could come and live in my sty with me!' said Polly. 'I should never feel lonely then.'

So she put her front feet up on the pram and spoke to the baby.

'You are so pretty and sweet! Do come and live with me, little darling!'

But the baby was afraid of the piglet, and she cried very loudly. The other children ran up and chased the piglet away.

'How dare you make our baby cry, you ugly, muddy little pig? Go away!'

Polly was afraid of the angry children, and she trotted off quickly. The children ran after her a little way.

'Shoo, ugly little pig!' they shouted. 'Don't you dare to come near our darling baby again. If you do, we'll tell the farmer!'

'I wish I wasn't so ugly,' said poor Polly Piglet. 'If only I had feathers like the hen and the duck. If only I had soft wool like the sheep, or brown hair like the pretty calves.'

She ran on, feeling very sad. Soon she came to a clothes-line, and on it were some clean clothes belonging to the baby in the pram.

Polly looked at them. 'I have such an ugly, bare, pink body. Now, if I had pretty clothes to wear, like that baby, I should look really lovely!' Then a naughty plan came into Polly's mind. 'I will knock down this post – and the line will fall down – and the clothes will come down with it – and I will dress myself up in them!'

So Polly Piglet knocked down the post, and the clean clothes fell down to the ground!

What a lot there were! Coats and frocks, woollen leggings and frilly bonnets, and a really lovely red silk sash. And then little Polly Piglet had a wonderful time! First she put on a blue woollen coat. She put her front legs through the sleeves.

Then she put on some fine long woollen leggings. They fitted her back legs very nicely.

Then she tied a red sash round her waist, with a big bow on top of her back. She did look nice!

Last of all she put on a big bonnet, and tied the strings under her chin.

Look at her. What a pretty little piglet she is! No wonder the curl has come back to her tail.

'Perhaps everyone will like me now!' said Polly Piglet, and trotted off by herself.

She really looked sweet. She was very careful not to go into any puddles because she didn't want to splash her lovely clothes. She didn't go near the hedge either, in case she caught her coat on the prickles.

'I am a very pretty little pig!' said Polly to herself.

Now, who should she meet, walking proudly along, but Mr Percy Pig! He

was big and round, and Polly Piglet was afraid of him.

She tried to hide in a corner, but Mr Percy Pig saw her.

'What a lovely piglet!' he grunted. 'And how nicely dressed! Grunt-grunt-grunt – I have never seen such a ladylike pig. Where do you come from?'

'From my sty,' said Polly. 'You see, I was lonely there, and I wanted someone to play with. But nobody likes me, and they all shoo me away.

'What a shame!' grunted kind Mr Percy Pig. 'I have always wanted a dear, pretty little wife like you. Come and live with me, and I will not let you be lonely any more.'

Oh, how happy Polly Piglet was to hear that! Now she really would have someone to love her, and to play such jolly games with her. She would never be lonely again.

She went off with Mr Percy Pig, and he told everyone how lovely she was. They met quite a lot of animals on their way to the sty.

'This is my pretty little wife,' said Mr Percy Pig to the lambs and the calves.

'This is Mrs Polly Pig, my dear little wife!' said Mr Percy Pig when they met the hen, chicks, duck and ducklings.

Everyone stared at Polly, so grand in her clothes, and they nodded and bowed politely.

'How do you do? We are so pleased to meet you! Do play with us sometimes,' they all said.

'Oh, I will, I will,' said Polly Piglet, happily. 'But I shan't be lonely now I have dear Mr Percy Pig to look after me.'

She trotted all through the farmyard in her new clothes, and even old

Dobbin, the horse, spoke to her. 'Good morning, my lady-pig, what a pleasure to see you looking so lovely!'

'I am really very proud of you,' said Mr Percy Pig to Polly.

And now little Polly Piglet is so happy. She can't possibly be lonely

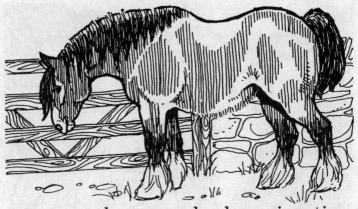

any more because she has nine tiny pink piglets of her very own to play with.

The hen brings her little chicks to see them every day. 'Cluck-cluck!' she says. 'Your piglets are very sweet.'

'Cheep-cheep!' say the chicks. 'We want to play with them.'

The duck brings her yellow ducklings. 'Quack-quack! What beautiful piglets!' she says, and all the ducklings run into the sty to talk to the piglets.

The four lambs come, too, and they put their little noses through the bars of the sty-gate. 'Oh, please, Mrs Polly Pig, will you let your piglets play with us this morning?' they bleat. 'Baa-aabaa, we do like them so!'

The two calves look over the gate and moo softly. 'What a beautiful family!' they say, gazing at them out of soft brown eyes. 'You're not lonely now, are you, Polly Piglet? You have so many piglets to play jolly games with!'

Even the children come and peep at the happy little family. They bring the baby and let her see the squealing piglets. She claps her hands and crows for joy.

'You don't feel unhappy now, do you, Polly?' the children say.

'Oh no. I'm the happiest pig in all the world, and I'm never lonely now!' says Polly. 'But I do wish I hadn't grown out of the lovely clothes I wore when I first met dear Mr Percy Pig!'

'Grunt-grunt! You looked very beautiful then,' says kind Mr Percy Pig, 'and you still look lovely to me, though now you only wear your skin, and have no red silk sash tied round your middle!'

Gillian Earns Some Money

One summer's day Gillian saw that the calendar in the dining-room had been altered to August. She stared at it for a minute and then she said:

'Oh dear me! Mummy's birthday is this month! And I've only got fifty pence in my money-box! Now what ever shall I do?'

'You can have some of *my* money,' said her little sister, Fiona.

'Thank you, Fiona, but *I* can't buy Mummy a present with *your* money,' said Gillian. 'I must get some more somehow.'

She thought and she thought, but she couldn't think of any way to earn money. But just then she heard her father say, 'Dear dear! The pony carriage is so dirty

71

again, and I've hardly time to clean it this morning!'

Gillian jumped up at once. 'Daddy, I want to earn fifty pence,' she said. 'Do you think if I helped you it would be worth fifty pence?'

'Yes, if you do it properly,' said her father. 'We'll go and start it now.'

Well, really it was more fun than work to help father clean the carriage! First they washed it all over and then they polished it. Soon the carriage began to shine and gleam.

There was quite a lot to do because the inside was dirty too. But at last it was all finished and it did look nice! Father was pleased.

'You have worked hard,' he said. 'Here is your fifty pence. I expect you are trying to save up for Mummy's birthday, aren't you?'

'Yes,' said Gillian. 'That makes one pound now.'

'If you go to Margaret next door I expect she could find you a job to do,' said Father. 'She is very busy today.'

Gillian went to Margaret. She was baking cakes. 'Why, Gillian,' she said, 'you are just the person I want to see! I came in from the garden in such a hurry this morning that I upset the peg-basket on the path, and it was pouring with rain so I couldn't stop to pick up the pegs. If you want to earn a pound, go and find them for me, will you, and wash them under the tap?'

'That's a nice job!' said Gillian. So off she went with the peg-basket. She hunted up the path and down the path and at last she found all the pegs. She took them to the garden tap and washed the mud carefully off each one. Then she set them in the sun to dry.

Margaret was pleased. She put a pound on the window-sill for Gillian. That went into her money-box too.

'That's two pounds!' said Gillian.

Just then her father called her. 'Have you seen these weeds in the lettuce-bed?' he said. 'See how the rain has brought them up! Are you busy?'

'No,' said Gillian. 'I will help you if you like.'

So very soon she was bending over the lettuce-bed pulling up the chickweed that had come up in the rain. How hard she worked!

'You're as good a gardener as I am!' said Father, after an hour. 'There's Mummy calling you now. Here's another fifty pence for your help. I'm very grateful.'

'Ooooh! That's two pounds fifty now!' said Gillian, and she ran indoors, pleased.

After dinner Mother said she was going out that afternoon, and she wondered if Gillian would feed the hens for her after tea. Gillian loved feeding the hens, so she said, 'Yes, of course!' at once. So after tea Gillian fed the hens, and gave them fresh water and fetched them some new cabbage stalks to play with. It was great fun.

Mother was pleased when she came home and found the hens so well fed and watered. She slipped something into Gillian's money-box, a pound coin, and a fifty pence piece too!

Gillian Earns Some Money

That's four pounds, thought Gillian, joyfully. 'Now I can buy Mummy that brooch I saw in the village shop, with a big M on it for Mother.'

So the next weekend, before she went out, she emptied her money-box and counted all her pound coins and fifty pences to make sure she had four pounds. And she had. She put all the money into her purse, tucked it into her pocket, and off she went.

It really was a lovely brooch. The M was made of a kind of pearly stuff that shone softly. The shopman packed the brooch into a little box with cotton-wool, and Gillian gave him her four pounds.

'Now I've got Mummy's birthday present,' she told Fiona when she got home. 'Would you like to see it? Look!'

77

Fiona liked it. Skipper liked it. Rusty liked it–and even the cats liked it, by the way they sniffed all over it.

But Mummy liked it the best of all! She wears it every morning on the front of her dress.

'Everybody knows you are Mother now, because you wear the letter M,' said Gillian. 'You don't know how hard I had to work to buy that brooch for you, Mummy, but I loved it.'

She did work hard, didn't she? But I expect you do the same sort of thing when *your* mother's birthday comes along, don't you!

Billy-Dog

A big dog lived next door to the twins. He was black and brown and he had such a stump of a tail that it was hardly big enough to wag.

'He's a silly dog,' said Jenny. 'He really is. He doesn't know any tricks, and he won't ever run after a stick or a ball.'

'He can't even sit up and beg when I show him a biscuit,' said Johnny. 'I've tried to make him, but he just falls over every time.'

'And he still hasn't learnt not to walk on the flower-beds,' said Jenny. 'He came in yesterday and walked all over ours. I think he's a stupid dog.'

'He's old,' said their mother. 'He can't be bothered to learn tricks now. He should have been taught long ago not to

79

walk on flower-beds, and to chase a ball–
he'll never learn now. But he's a nice old
fellow.'

'He's dull,' said Johnny. 'He won't
play, he won't run.'

'The only thing he does is to go out
looking for rabbits,' said Jenny. 'Granny
told me. But she said he never, never
catches one and she is sure that if a
rabbit chased him, he would run away!'

Mother laughed. 'Well, don't bother
with old Billy-Dog if you think he's silly
and won't play. I'm quite sure he doesn't
want to bother himself with *you!*'

'We won't notice him at all,' said
Johnny. 'He's just too silly for words.'

So they didn't bother with Billy-Dog
any more. They didn't call him to go with
them when they went for a walk. They

80

didn't bounce a ball for him or throw him a stick. And Billy-Dog didn't take any notice of them either. He just lay in his front garden, or trotted off to look for rabbits in the woods, and didn't even wag his stump of a tail when the twins came by.

One day the twins went off to the woods to pick bluebells. Their mother had said she would like some because they smelt so lovely.

The woods were full of bluebells. They shone like blue pools between the trees, and there were so many that not even when the twins had picked a big bunch did the bluebells seem any less.

'We could pick a million and they wouldn't be missed!' said Jenny. 'Oh Johnny, aren't they lovely? They look like patches of blue sky fallen down in the woods.'

The twins wandered on and on. Johnny wanted to find a white bluebell because it was lucky, so they looked everywhere.

'It must be getting late,' said Jenny, at last.

'I don't know the time, but my tummy tells me it's nearly dinner time. I'm very, very hungry.'

'Well, let's go home then,' said Johnny, and he turned down a path. 'Come on. I'm hungry too.'

But they hadn't gone very far before Johnny stopped. 'This isn't right,' he said, in alarm. 'I don't know this path!'

'Oh dear! We aren't lost, are we?' said Jenny. 'I don't want to be lost.'

But they *were* lost! They went down this path and that path, but always they came to the end and found themselves even deeper in the wood. 'These paths are just rabbit-paths!' said Johnny, at last. 'They only lead to rabbit-holes.'

'Johnny, shall we be like the Babes in the Wood and have to go to sleep and be covered up with leaves?' asked Jenny. 'Oh, please find the right way.'

But Johnny couldn't, and soon the twins stood under the big trees, with Jenny crying and Johnny looking very scared.

'Listen! There's a noise!' said Johnny, suddenly. They both listened.

'It's not a nice noise,' said Jenny, tears falling down her cheeks. 'It's a nasty snuffly noise. It sounds like a big animal. Let's hide.'

But before they could hide, the big animal came round a bush, nose to the ground, snuffling loudly as he went.

And will you believe it, it was Billy-Dog! There he was, standing in front of the children, just as surprised to see them as they were to see him!

Jenny flung herself on him. 'Billy-Dog! Oh, I'm so glad to see you! Are you lost too? Stay with us and guard us, Billy-Dog!'

Billy-Dog saw that Jenny was unhappy. He licked her face with his big tongue.

Johnny took hold of his collar. 'Don't go away and leave us!' he said. 'Let's all be lost together! Then when people come to look for you and for us, they'll find us all.'

Billy-Dog pulled away from Johnny. He didn't like to be held by his collar. He got himself free and trotted away. Johnny ran after him. 'Don't go, don't go!' he cried.

Billy-Dog stopped, but he trotted on again as soon as Johnny came up to him. Then when he was some way in front he stopped once more and looked round. His stump of a tail wagged itself.

The twins ran to him, but again he trotted away in front. He wouldn't let them catch him. It was most annoying.

'He's so *silly!*' said Jenny. 'He just won't understand that we want him with us. I feel safe with him.'

'He'll lead us deeper into the wood,' said Johnny. 'We'll get more lost than ever. But we'd better follow him, Jenny, because I feel safe when he's near, too.'

So they followed Billy-Dog, and when they got left behind he stopped and waited for them. Then on he went again.

Right through the wood they went, and at last they came out into a field. Across the field went Billy-Dog, and under a gate. 'Oh dear, wherever is he taking us now?' said Johnny. 'We must be miles away from home!'

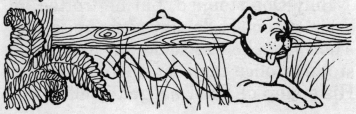

And then, when they had climbed over the gate into a lane, Jenny gave a shout.

'Johnny! JOHNNY! This is the lane that leads to our back-garden! It is, it is! We're nearly home!'

So they were! They just had to run up the lane, and go into the gate at the end of their garden and race up to the house!

'You *are* late!' said Mother, meeting them at the door. 'I was getting worried. I thought you were lost.'

'We were,' said Johnny. 'But Billy-Dog was in the woods and he brought us all the way home. Fancy, Mummy, he knew the way quite well, though we didn't. And he was very kind, he kept waiting for us to catch up with him.'

'He's very clever,' said Jenny. 'Much cleverer than we are. *He* wasn't lost at all.'

'Dear me, I thought you said he was silly,' said Mother.

'We made a mistake,' said Johnny. 'We were the silly ones! Billy-Dog is old and wise. I shall take my pocket-money to the butcher this afternoon and buy him a juicy bone.'

So the twins bought a big bone for Billy-Dog and took it to him. He was surprised and pleased. He wagged his stump of a tail and gave a little bark.

'He's saying thank you,' said Johnny. 'Billy-Dog, we think you're clever, not silly, after all. Please will you take us for a walk next time you go to the woods?'

'Woof,' said Billy-Dog, just as if he understood. And do you know, the very next day when he wanted to go and look for rabbits, he went to fetch the twins, so that they could go with him!

'I think it's very nice of him!' said Jenny. I think it was, too, don't you?

Mr Tweeky's Magic Pockets

Mr Tweeky was a round, fat little man, with the jolliest smile you could imagine. He was dreadfully poor, and he lived all by himself in a round, fat little cottage at the end of Dum-Dum Village. He always wore a red coat that buttoned tightly up to his neck, and had two very deep pockets in it. In one of them he kept his dinner, and in the other he put things like handkerchiefs, money and tickets.

One day Mr Tweeky started off to look for work. He had a very dull dinner wrapped up in paper in one of his pockets, and he wasn't looking forward to eating it. He hoped perhaps he would be able to find some work, and then he might buy a nice bit of cheese to go with his dry bread.

He was just going down the road when he heard someone call 'Help! Help!' He looked to see who it was, and saw an old woman waving to him out of a window.

'A pipe has burst in the bathroom, and the house is being swamped!' she cried. 'Come and help me, do!'

Mr Tweeky rushed into the house. He took his coat off in the hall, and hung it up, with his hat. Then he turned up his shirt sleeves and tore upstairs.

Dear me! What a sight he saw! The water was pouring out of a hole in a pipe and had soaked everything.

'I'll put my thumb on it whilst you go for a plumber,' said Mr Tweeky. 'Hurry up, or you'll have to swim!'

'Thank you, thank you,' said the old woman, and she ran downstairs. Mr Tweeky waited for about twenty minutes with his thumb on the hole, and then the old woman came back with a plumber who quickly stopped the water and said he would put in a new piece of pipe.

'I'm very grateful to you,' said the old woman to Mr Tweeky. 'Thank you so much.'

'Don't mention it,' said Mr Tweeky politely. 'I'm glad to have been of use. I'll just pop downstairs now and get my coat.'

So down he popped and put on his coat and hat once more. Then out into the street he went, whistling cheerily, glad that he had been able to do someone a good turn.

'Hallo, Tweeky!' said a friend of his.
'Where have you been?'

Mr Tweeky told his friend about
the burst pipe.

'You're a very good chap,' said his
friend Higgle, who was very fond of Mr
Tweeky. 'I wish you could get a bit of
good luck. You are always poor, and
you never have any treats.'

'Ah,' said Mr Tweeky, sighing, 'I
wish the good old days of fairies would
come back again. Then I'd wish a few

wishes, and get everything I wanted!'

Higgle walked along with Mr Tweeky, and when dinner-time came they sat down together on a sunny bank to eat their meal. Mr Tweeky's friend had cold sausage and new bread and a nice piece of cake.

'What have *you* got, Tweeky?' he asked.

'Only stale dry bread, and not very much of that!' said Mr Tweeky, sighing. 'I wish I'd got cold sausage and new bread like you. And for my pudding I'd like a nice piece of jam-roll.'

He put his hand in his pocket and pulled out his dinner. It was wrapped up in paper. Mr Tweeky unwrapped it – and then he stared as if he couldn't believe his eyes!

'Buttons and buttercups!' he cried. 'Look here! Here's my wish come true, I do declare! Cold sausage! New bread! And – oh! The finest piece of jam-roll I ever saw! Why, there's magic about still!'

Mr Tweeky's friend stared with his eyes and mouth wide open. He thought it was a most surprising thing.

Mr Tweeky ate up his dinner with joy. He had never had such a delicious one before. The jam-roll was perfectly lovely, and the sausage was really tasty.

'You've got jam all over your nose and mouth,' said Higgle. 'You do look funny.'

Mr Tweeky dived into his other pocket for his handkerchief – but when he brought it out he was lost in astonishment.

'Look at that!' he shouted in delight.

'My own handkerchief is an old, torn red cotton one – and it's changed into this lovely blue silk one! Buttons and buttercups, there's certainly magic about today!'

'That's a wonderful thing,' said Higgle. 'Well, Tweeky, I always said you deserved a bit of good luck if ever anyone did – and now that you've got it, I'm glad.'

Mr Tweeky beamed all over his round, fat little face. He was so pleased. He wiped the jam off his nose, and put his handkerchief away again.

'Well, I must go on now,' he said. 'I heard that there was a gardener wanted at the other end of the village. I must go and see if I can get the job.'

'I'm going that way, too,' said Higgle, 'but I'm going to take the bus – it's so far to walk.'

'I haven't enough money for that,' said Mr Tweeky, putting his hand into his pocket. 'Look, I've only got five pence!'

He pulled out a coin – and my, didn't he stare! It was a pound!'

'Look at that now!' he said. 'There's my five pence changed into a pound! Did you ever see anything like it?'

Higgle was more surprised than ever. He took the pound and bit it to see if it was good, and it was.

'Now you'll be able to catch the bus,' he said. 'The fare is only ten pence.'

So they both caught the bus, and Mr Tweeky enjoyed the ride very much, for

it was a long time since he had been in a bus.

'Would you like a toffee?' asked Higgle. 'I've got one to spare.'

'Oh, that's very kind of you,' said Mr Tweeky. 'I wish I'd a few to offer you, but I haven't a single one.'

'I say! Feel in your pockets and see if you've got any now!' said Higgle excitedly. So Mr Tweeky felt solemnly in his pockets – and brought out a whole bag of assorted toffees!

'Well, I never!' he said. 'This is the loveliest day I've ever had, Higgle. My luck certainly *is* in.'

'See what else you've got in your pockets,' said Higgle. 'Perhaps everything has changed into something better.'

So Mr Tweeky looked – and he was *so* astonished at what he found. First there was a very nice pair of gloves, with fur inside. Then there was another handkerchief, made of yellow silk. There were two lovely pencils, and a fine fountain-pen. There was a notebook, a purse with five pounds in, and, last of all, a little case.

'What's in the case?' asked Higgle, bending over to see. 'My, Tweeky, there's certainly plenty of magic about you today!'

Mr Tweeky opened the case. Inside there were a lot of visiting-cards.

'Oh, fancy!' he cried. 'These are cards! I expect they'll all have my name on! Buttons and buttercups! How grand I shall be!'

He took out one of the cards and looked at it – and then he looked again – and then he rubbed his eyes and looked a third time.

'Look, Higgle,' he said to his friend. 'Do you see my name there?'

Higgle looked. 'No!' he said in surprise. 'It's someone else's name! It says

Mr Joseph Hubble-Bubble! Now, whatever does that mean?'

'Well, my name's Tweeky, isn't it?' said Mr Tweeky, puzzled. 'Something's gone wrong with the magic. I wonder why they put Hubble-Bubble.'

'There's a Mr Hubble-Bubble lives in the village somewhere,' said Higgle. 'I've heard of him. I wonder why his name is on the cards in your pocket. This is very funny.'

Then a really terrible thought came to Mr Tweeky. He turned quite pale. He looked down at his red coat, and turned paler still. He quite frightened Higgle.

'What's the matter?' said his friend. 'Are you ill, Tweeky?'

'No,' said Tweeky in a faint voice. 'But, oh, Higgle! I don't believe these pockets are magic, after all. I–I–I–'

'What! Tell me quickly!' cried Higgle.

'I–I–I–believe I've got someone else's coat on,' said poor Mr Tweeky. 'I hardly dare to look, Higgle. Just tell me, is there a big patch on the right shoulder?'

Higgle looked. 'No,' he said. 'There's no patch at all.'

'Is there a button gone from the right cuff?' asked Mr Tweeky.

'No, there's a button there all right,' said Higgle.

'Then it's n-n-n-not my coat,' said Mr Tweeky. 'Oh, what shall I do!'

'But how could you have got someone else's?' asked Higgle, puzzled.

'Why, do you remember that I told you how I went in to help that old woman with her burst pipe this morning?' said Mr Tweeky. 'Well, I took my coat and hat off and hung them in the hall. When I came downstairs to put them on again, I must have put on someone else's red coat. And that's

why all those lovely things were in the pockets!'

'Then the sausage and jam-roll weren't magic!' said Higgle. 'They were someone else's.'

'Yes,' said Mr Tweeky mournfully. 'And I've eaten them. And we've eaten all the sweets. And there's jam all over the handkerchief. And I've spent some of the money. Whatever shall I do?'

'You'll have to go back and own up,' said Higgle sorrowfully. 'I'm ever so sorry for you, Tweeky; I really *did* think you'd got a bit of good luck today – and it's turned out to be *bad* luck after all!'

Mr Tweeky stopped the bus and got down. Higgle jumped down too.

'I'll come back with you,' he said comfortingly. 'I'll tell the old woman that you thought it was magic, and didn't know you were eating anyone else's dinner.'

So the two friends walked all the way back to the old woman's house. It was evening when they reached there, and

when at last they stood outside the house, they heard a voice talking loudly inside one of the front rooms.

'Come on, we must go in and tell Mr Hubble-Bubble what you've done,' whispered Higgle. So the two went up the path and knocked at the front door

'My lovely dinner had changed into dry bread!' said the voice. 'And my toffees were gone! I hadn't got my pencils or my fountain-pen, and even my new gloves and nice silk handker-chiefs had disappeared. Someone must have put a bad spell on me, that's what *I* think! Oh, dear me, how horrid it is! I really do feel most unhappy!'

The old woman came to open it and bade Tweeky and Higgle come inside out of the cold. They followed her into a cosy room where a little old man, just as round as Tweeky, was walking up and down.

'Please,' said Mr Tweeky in a small voice, 'I've come to say that owing to a mistake, and our coats being so much alike, I took yours this morning and left my own.'

'Bless us all!' cried the little old man in joy. 'Then there isn't a spell on me after all! It was *your* dinner I found, and *your* red handkerchief I used! Well, well, well!'

'I'm sorry to say that I thought I had some magic about me,' said Mr Tweeky. 'So I decided your dinner was mine changed into something better. And I'm also sorry to say that I've

eaten your sweets and spent some of your money, and made your blue handkerchief jammy.'

The little old lady began to laugh. Then Mr Hubble-Bubble began to smile too, and soon he was chuckling loudly.

'This is very funny,' he said. 'Very funny indeed.'

'*I* don't think it is,' said poor Mr Tweeky. 'I can't pay you back for your dinner or sweets, because I've only got five pence in the world, and I'm out of work.'

'Then it isn't funny at all,' said the old man, looking grave. 'But, tell me, how did you get my coat?'

Mr Tweeky told him.

'Oh, so you're the kind person who came and helped my wife this morning,' said the old man. 'Well, now, I need a really good, hard-working gardener, someone who will look after my wife as well when things go wrong in the house. Would you like the job?'

Mr Tweeky could hardly speak for

joy. It was just the sort of work he loved. Higgle spoke up for his friend, and said what a kind, helpful fellow he was; so the old man engaged him on the spot.

'So it *was* my lucky day, after all!' said Mr Tweeky, as he struggled into his old coat, and gave up the one he had

been wearing. 'I'm very happy again, now.'

And off he marched with Higgle, both of them as merry as blackbirds!

The Talking Teapot

Once upon a time, when Dimble-Dumble was walking across the common, he saw a yellow teapot sitting in a gorse bush. The pixie was very surprised, for teapots do not usually sit in bushes.

It was a very nice teapot. Dimble-Dumble looked at it all round. It wasn't cracked, like the one he had at home. Its spout wasn't broken either. It was a very good teapot, and there was nothing the matter with it at all.

'Mine's very old,' said Dimble-Dumble. 'Mine is a disgraceful teapot. This one is a good one, and a lovely colour. I shall take it home with me.'

Now that was naughty of him, because he knew quite well that it must

belong to someone. In fact, he felt certain that it belonged to the Yellow Gnome who lived not far away, and had yellow tables and chairs, yellow plates and cups, and probably a yellow teapot to match. But Dimble-Dumble wouldn't think of that. He wanted the teapot, and he meant to have it.

So he lifted it out of the gorse bush and put it under his coat. He ran all the way home with it, and when he got there he took the teapot out and looked at it. It certainly was a very fine one.

Dimble-Dumble took down his old teapot, and threw it on the floor, where it broke into a hundred pieces.

'There!' he said. 'Now you can go into the dustbin, old teapot. You're done for! I'll use my new yellow teapot, and make everyone very jealous!'

He put it up on the shelf, and then cleared away the broken pieces of the old teapot. As he was doing this, his friend Peter Pie came in.

'I say, Dimble-Dumble,' he said. 'Will you lend me fifty pence till tomorrow?'

Now Dimble-Dumble hated lending anybody anything. So he shook his head.

'I haven't even ten pence!' he said.

Then something queer happened. A loud, deep voice suddenly spoke in the pixie's kitchen.

'Dimble-Dumble's mean!' said the voice. 'Ho, mean Dimble-Dumble!'

The pixie and his friend looked all round in surprise. There was no one there at all. Dimble-Dumble went red, for he knew that the voice spoke the truth. He *was* being mean.

'Ho!' began the voice again. 'Ho! Dimble-Dumble's mean!'

The pixie hurriedly took ten pence from his pocket and gave it to his friend.

117

'Here you are,' he said. 'Now run away, because I'm busy.'

Peter Pie went out, much astonished. As soon as he had gone, Dimble-Dumble had a good hunt round his kitchen to see who had spoken. He felt certain that some gnome or elf must be hiding there. But he could find nobody. The voice didn't speak again, but just as he passed the shelf where he kept his china he heard a deep chuckle. Dimble-Dumble hunted all along the shelf, but he still couldn't see anyone. He didn't for one minute guess that it was the yellow teapot!

After a time he gave it up and began to get his dinner ready. Soon there came a knock at the door, and a grey rabbit looked in.

'Dimble-Dumble, could you come and help me to pick my peas?' he asked. 'I'm going to do them this afternoon. I'd be very glad of your help.'

Now it was a hot day, and Dimble-Dumble didn't want to work hard. So he shook his head.

'I'm sorry,' he said. 'But I'm afraid I can't.'

Then the loud, deep voice spoke again.

'Dimble-Dumble's lazy,' said the voice. 'Ho, lazy Dimble-Dumble!'

The rabbit stared round in surprise, but could see no one. The pixie went very red.

'I'll come and help you this afternoon, Bobtail,' he said in a hurry. 'Now run off, for I'm busy!'

The rabbit went away, very puzzled. Dimble-Dumble glared round his kitchen, but it was no use. He could *not* see who had spoken. The yellow teapot chuckled deeply, and made him jump – but still he didn't guess where the voice came from.

He ate his dinner, and then went off to help Bobtail to pick his peas. After that he came home again, and began to get ready for a tea-party he was having that afternoon. He buttered some biscuits, iced some buns, made some jam sandwiches, and took a ginger cake out of a tin. Then he set out plates, cups and saucers, took down the yellow teapot, and put the kettle on to boil. By the time four o'clock came he was quite ready for his visitors.

In they came, Peter Pie and Pipkin, Gillie and Poppo, Chiffle-Chuffle and Tiptoe. They said good afternoon politely, and sat down to tea. Dimble-

Dumble put some tea into the yellow teapot, poured boiling water in, and the tea was made.

Soon they were all eating and talking merrily. Pipkin asked Dimble-Dumble where he had got his lovely new teapot from.

'It was a birthday present,' said Dimble-Dumble untruthfully, for he didn't want to say how he had found it.

'Dimble-Dumble's a story-teller!' said the teapot in a loud, deep voice. 'Ho, story-telling Dimble-Dumble!'

Nobody knew where the voice had come from. Everyone except the pixie thought that one of the guests at the table had spoken the strange words. They looked at one another in silence, wondering who it was.

'Ho,' began the voice again, 'Dimble-Dumble's a story-teller!'

'I found the teapot in a bush,' said Dimble-Dumble quickly. 'It wasn't a birthday present. Don't let's talk about it any more.'

So his guests politely changed the subject and talked about other things. But the teapot wouldn't let them. It began to talk too, and it had such a very loud voice that it drowned everyone else.

'DIMBLE-DUMBLE IS MEAN,' it said. 'HO, DIMBLE-DUMBLE IS LAZY, TOO, AND DIMBLE-DUMBLE TELLS STORIES! HO, MEAN DIMBLE-DUMBLE, LAZY DIMBLE-DUMBLE, STORY-TELLING DIMBLE-DUMBLE!'

'Who's saying all these things?' asked Peter Pie in great surprise.

'*I'm* not!' said Pipkin.

'Nor am I!' said Gillie.

'And *we're* not!' said Poppo, Chiffle-Chuffle and Tiptoe, all together.

'HO, HO!' chuckled the teapot, and it waggled its spout at them all. 'HO, HO!'

'Look! It's the teapot!' cried everyone. 'It's alive! Ooh! It's a magic teapot! Dimble-Dumble, how foolish you were to take it from the bush when it didn't belong to you!'

The little pixie was very miserable. He sat and looked at the teapot, wondering what it was going to say next. He didn't have to wait long, for it began to say all sorts of unkind things about him, and he went very red indeed, for most of them were true.

His friends soon went away, for the tea-party was quite spoilt. Dimble-Dumble was left alone with the teapot, which began to make faces at him. It was a very ill-behaved pot.

'I'll go and ask the Yellow Gnome if it's his,' said Dimble-Dumble. 'Then perhaps he will have it back.'

So off he went and knocked at the door of the Yellow Gnome's bright yellow house. The gnome himself came to the door, and asked what the pixie wanted.

'Yellow Gnome,' began Dimble-Dumble, 'I found a yellow teapot in a gorse bush this morning, and took it home. I know it was very wrong of me. It is a very rude teapot, and says all sorts of unkind things. Will you please take it back?'

The Yellow Gnome slapped his knees, threw back his head, and laughed a very loud laugh. When he had finished he shook his head.

'No,' he said. '*I* don't want it back! I threw it away because it said such rude things about *me*! You keep it, Dimble-Dumble! Much good may it do you!'

He slammed the door, and poor Dimble-Dumble went home wishing hard that he hadn't touched that teapot.

I'll smash it to pieces, he thought. Then that will be the end of it!

So when he got home he took hold of the teapot and flung it hard on the ground. But it didn't break! Instead, it bounced high into the air and hit the pixie on the nose!

He couldn't break it however he tried. Even when he hit it with a hammer it wouldn't break. So then he took it to the bottom of his garden and threw it away as far as he could. But it came back! It hopped up the garden path, in at the kitchen door, and put itself in the sink to be washed. Whatever was Dimble-Dumble to do?

He began to cry. He tried to break the teapot again. He put it into the dustbin, but it threw off the lid and came back to the kitchen. He tried to drown it, but it simply loved the water and bobbed up and down like a boat.

So in the end the poor little pixie had to wash it, and put it back on the shelf.

'Ho, ho!' it said. 'Ho, ho!' and then with another deep chuckle it went to sleep.

But what a nuisance it was to Dimble-Dumble all the rest of the week! Every time he did anything mean or greedy, selfish or horrid, the teapot spoke about it. There was no stopping it; and it had such a loud voice that everyone heard what it said.

Soon Dimble-Dumble found that the only way to stop it talking was to be careful never to do anything wrong or horrid. If he told the truth, was helpful and kind, and never did anything mean, the teapot was silent. It only spoke when it could say something unkind. There it sat on the shelf beside a new blue teapot, which the pixie had bought because he wouldn't use the yellow one.

Then one day Dimble-Dumble had an idea.

'I found it in a gorse bush!' he said. 'If I throw it into one, perhaps it will stay there! When the Yellow Gnome threw it there, it stayed, and didn't go back to him. Perhaps it will stop there if *I* throw it into a prickly gorse bush!'

He took the teapot and went to the common. He chose a very big, prickly bush and then threw the teapot right into the middle of it. It tried to get out, but it couldn't.

'Ha!' said the pixie in delight. 'Ha! Mean teapot, unkind teapot, horrid teapot! Stay there until someone else finds you!'

He hurried home, singing happily. Oh, it was lovely to have got rid of that nasty talking teapot!

But it's taught me a few lessons, thought Dimble-Dumble, putting the kettle on to boil. It's taught me to tell the truth, to be unselfish, and not to be lazy. So really I ought to be grateful to it, though it *was* a horrid teapot! I wonder who will find it. Well, they'd better leave it alone, or they will be very sorry!

Nobody has found it yet, because the gorse bush is very thick and prickly – but if you *should* happen to see a yellow teapot on the common, take my advice and leave it alone!

How Lucky They Were!

'Why don't you two go nutting?' said
Mother to Mary and David. 'Take a
basket each and go down Hazel Lane to
the woods. The nuts will be ripe now.'

'Oh *yes*–that would be fun!' said the
children, and they found their baskets
and set off together. It was a sunny
autumn day, just right for picking nuts.

They went down the lane and came to
the woods. Hazel trees grew there by the
dozen. Nobody was about at all.

'That's funny! You'd think there
would be other children here, picking
nuts too,' said Mary.

'Well, look, Mary, there *aren't* any
nuts!' said David, staring at one tree
after another. 'That's why there's
nobody here! They've all been picked.

No wonder the shops are full of hazel nuts now. I expect other children have been here, picked the nuts and sold them.'

'Oh, what a pity there aren't any left for us,' said Mary, and she began to hunt under the trees. But no, except for two bad nuts she couldn't find any to put into her basket at all.

'Look – quick, look, Mary. There's a little red squirrel!' whispered David suddenly. The children stood very still and looked at the beautiful little creature. He hadn't seen them. He came scampering down a tree, and bounded about on the grass, his lovely bushy tail out behind him. He played about, and then sat up just as if he were listening.

What had he heard? Yes, the farm dog! The collie came rushing up, and suddenly made a rush at the little red squirrel. The little creature scampered to a tree and leapt up the trunk, on to a bough.

But the bough was rotten and gave under the squirrel's light weight. There was no bough below for him to drop to, and he fell to the ground. He was up again in a moment, but the farm dog was on him!

David gave a yell. 'Hey! Let go of that squirrel, Rover. Do you hear? Let go! Bad dog, let go!'

Rover was an obedient dog and he liked the twins. He dropped the scared squirrel at once, put his tail down and ran off. 'I didn't mean any harm!' he seemed to say. 'I really didn't!'

The squirrel lay where it was, too scared to move. The children went up quietly. Mary put out a hand. 'Little thing! You're all right, aren't you? Rover didn't hurt you, did he?'

The squirrel's heart was racing fast with shock. He allowed Mary to pick him up and cuddle him against her. 'He feels so little and soft, David,' whispered Mary, her eyes shining. 'I do love him. Will he be all right?'

'He's not hurt, just frightened,' said David, stroking the bushy tail gently. 'Oh, he's off and away!'

The squirrel suddenly felt better and leapt right out of Mary's arms. He bounded over the grass, as light as a feather. He looked back at them.

'Let's see where he goes,' said David. 'He's not a bit afraid of us. Perhaps he will show us his home.'

They followed the little red squirrel, who bounded off in front, sometimes running up a tree and down again, but always waiting for them. At last the children found themselves in a deeper part of the wood–and there, in front of them, were three big hazel trees.

'The nuts! LOOK at the nuts on them!' said David, excitedly. 'Oh Mary, we can fill our baskets full!'

The squirrel ran up one of the trees and made a little chattering noise. 'He says he's led us here to his special nut-trees,' said Mary, laughing. 'All right, little friend, we'll help ourselves, thank you!'

And, with the squirrel bounding all about them, they picked the lovely brown nuts in their greeny-brown sheaths, and put them into their baskets. They were soon full!

'Time to go home,' said David. 'Come on, we can't get even one more nut into our baskets, Mary. Goodbye, squirrel, and thank you very much!'

But the squirrel came with them right to Hazel Lane. Then he scampered up a tree and disappeared.

'What lovely nuts!' said Mother, when they arrived home with their baskets full. 'How clever you are to find such a lot!'

'Not clever, just lucky to have a friend to show us the best trees,' said David. 'I'll take you to meet him tomorrow, Mummy. His name is Frisky Squirrel!'

Take us with you, David. *We'd* like to meet him too!

The Wizard's Needle

There was once a wizard called So-So, who had a wonderful needle. He had only to speak to it and it would start sewing anything he wanted.

If he said, 'Needle, make me a bag,' it would make one.

If he said, 'Needle, make me a coat,' it would at once set to work to make him one out of any old rag.

Now one day Curly-Toes the pixie wanted some sacks for his potatoes. He couldn't afford to buy any, so he thought he would make them out of some old pieces of carpet that he had got. But when he had finished making one sack, he was very tired indeed, for he hated sewing.

If only I could borrow So-So's needle,

he thought, how fine that would be! I should only say "Needle, make me a sack" and it would make me one at once. All I should have to do would be to sit and watch it!

He made up his mind to go to wizard So-So's and ask him for the loan of his magic needle. So he put on his hat and set out. He banged at So-So's door, and the wizard opened it.

'Will you lend me your magic needle?' asked Curly-Toes.

'Certainly not,' said So-So. 'I never lend it to anyone. It is far too valuable.'

He slammed the door and left Curly-Toes on the step, frowning hard.

The pixie was setting off home again when he happened to catch sight of the needle on a table just inside So-So's kitchen window.

Ho! he thought. There's the needle itself! What's to prevent me from taking it and using it without the wizard knowing? I can easily put it back again when I have finished with it, and he won't be any the wiser!

With that the naughty pixie slipped his hand through the open window, picked up the needle, and ran off! It wasn't long before he was home again.

He took all the pieces of old carpet and laid them in a row on the floor. Then he put the magic needle in the middle of them.

'Needle, make me some sacks!' he said.

At once the little needle got busy. It jumped to a piece of carpet, and in a trice it had sewn one piece into a fine sack.

There was a long thread always sticking out of the needle and it used this to sew the sack together. It was really wonderful to watch.

Curly-Toes enjoyed it all thoroughly.

It was fine to sit down at the table and see the needle doing all his hard work. He would have plenty of strong sacks for his potatoes.

In five minutes the needle had used up all the pieces of carpet and had made six good sacks.

Curly-Toes waited for it to put itself quietly down beside them, then he meant to pick it up again and take it back to So-So's house.

But the needle didn't stop sewing! To Curly-Toes' great surprise it whipped up the lovely new rug on the floor and began to make a sack of that too!

'Hey!' said Curly-Toes, angrily. 'Stop, needle! That's my new rug! Don't spoil it! I don't want any more sacks now.'

The needle took no notice at all. It just went on sewing the rug into a sack. Curly-Toes rushed up to it and tried to

stop it. It pricked him hard on the finger and he howled with pain.

'Oh, you horrid needle!' he wept. 'Why don't you stop when you're told to? Stop, I tell you, stop!'

The needle still took no notice. It finished making a sack of the rug and then whipped down one of Curly-Toes' pretty red curtains and began to make that into a sack too.

The pixie couldn't bear it. He had made the curtains himself and he wasn't going to have them all spoilt.

He took a pair of pincers and went softly up to the needle. He suddenly pounced on it and caught it in the pincers. But it wasn't any good at all!

The needle slipped out quite easily and gave the pixie such a jab in the arm that he danced round the room in pain.

The needle took down the other curtain and made a sack of that too. Then it hopped on to the table and Curly-Toes gave a cry of rage.

It was going to make his lovely blue table-cloth into a sack as well!

'You shan't, you shan't!' he cried. 'I had it for my birthday and you shan't spoil it!'

He climbed on to the table and sat himself firmly down in the middle of the cloth to stop the needle from making it into a sack. But it wasn't a bit of good!

In a trice, the cloth was being sewn into a sack – and, oh dear me, what was happening?

Curly-Toes suddenly found himself sewn tightly into the sack too! The needle pulled the neck of the sack tight and sewed it carefully all the way round. Then it flew out of the window!

Poor Curly-Toes! He sat in the middle of the table, sewn tightly into a sack made of his blue table-cloth.

He struggled and wriggled, shouted and cried. But he couldn't get out of that sack!

Soon his friends heard his cries and they came running to his aid. How they

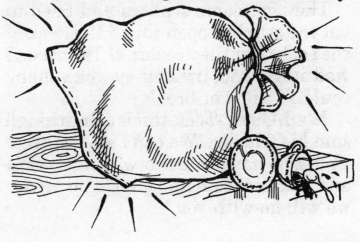

laughed to see the pixie in such a fix!

They got some scissors and tried to cut the stitches open round the neck of the sack. But they couldn't! The thread was magic and, try as they would, they couldn't cut it or break it.

'Well, Curly-Toes, this is a fine thing!' said his friends. 'We can't set you free! You will have to go to wizard So-So's and ask him to help you. Come along, we will go with you.'

So poor Curly-Toes was helped off the table and then he hopped slowly out of his front door, for it was impossible to walk in the sack.

He could do nothing but jump.

He kept tumbling over and, really, it was the funniest sight, though the pixie didn't think so.

At last he arrived at the wizard's house, and So-So opened the door. How he laughed to see the pixie in a table-cloth sack!

'Yes, I know what you've done!' he said. 'I saw you take my needle, but I knew it would punish you, so I didn't say anything. How are you going to get out of that sack?'

'Do please help me!' begged the pixie.

'Certainly not,' said the wizard. 'You got yourself into this fix, so you must get out of it yourself too.'

'Oh, do help him, So-So,' begged all Curly-Toes' friends. 'He is very, very sorry.'

'Well, if I get you out of the sack, will you come and weed my garden every

day for a week?' the wizard asked Curly-Toes.

Now the pixie hated weeding, but he couldn't do anything else but agree. So he said he would. Then So-So fetched a pair of magic scissors and – snip-snip! The stitches were all cut, and Curly-Toes was free!

Off he went home and spent the rest of the day trying to undo the stitches in his rug and curtains.

He went to bed a very sad pixie.

Then every day for a week he set off to weed the wizard's garden and, by the end of that time, he had learnt his lesson.

'I'll never, never borrow anything without asking!' he vowed. And, as far as I know, he never did!

What a Surprise!

Harry had a lovely little car that he pedalled up and down the garden, and sometimes down the lane.

It had a red body and yellow wheels, and the seat was big enough for two in front. There were two lamps, but no hooter, which was a pity. All cars had horns or hooters, and Harry did wish his had one.

One day he pedalled out of the back gate into the lane at the bottom of the garden. He came to a little path that led into the wood.

'It's wide enough for you, little car,' said Harry. 'So we'll go down it. What a pity I haven't a hooter so that you could hoot when rabbits get in our way!'

Now, not very long after that a

strange thing happened. Harry heard the noise of a bicycle bell ringing behind him – tinga-linga-ling! Tinga-linga-ling!

Who was this riding in the woods? Harry turned round in his car to see. Goodness gracious! It was a peculiar little man with funny pointed ears, riding a green bicycle at a furious pace!

'Get out of my way,' shouted the man, and Harry pulled his car aside just in time. The bicycle scraped the paint on his car as it raced by.

'Hey! What's up?' shouted Harry, but the funny little man was gone. Then Harry heard someone else shouting.

'Stop him! Stop that thief!'

And up ran another little fellow. He had pointed ears too, and a long beard. Harry thought he looked just like a brownie. Perhaps he was one! How wonderful it would be if he really met a brownie!

'I say! Why didn't you stop that fellow?' said the little man, quite out of breath. 'He came into my sweet-shop just now – the one I keep in Foxglove Dell, you know – and took a pocketful of my sweets.'

153

'Oh dear, I'm so sorry,' said Harry. 'Who are you?'

'Brownie Longbeard,' said the little fellow. 'I've got an idea! Let me get into your car. We can chase that bad brownie and catch him then.'

'Get in,' said Harry, feeling very excited. And in got the brownie. Harry began to pedal fast down the path. They came to a surprised rabbit, and the brownie leaned out of the car and shouted to him.

'Hey, Bunny! Have you seen a brownie on a green bicycle going by?'

'Yes. He nearly knocked me over,' said the rabbit. 'He went down that path over there.'

Longbeard and Harry set off again – but even though Harry pedalled as hard as he could, it wasn't fast enough for Longbeard.

'Let *me* take the steering-wheel, and pedal the car,' he said. 'I can go as fast as lightning!'

So the two changed places – but dear me, Longbeard pedalled so hard and the car shot along so fast that Harry was frightened!

'Stop! You nearly bumped into that tree!' he cried. 'Stop, Longbeard.'

Longbeard stopped. 'Sorry,' he said. 'Would you like to get out and walk back home? I'll go on by myself and catch that thief, and bring your car back afterwards. I know where you live.'

'I think I *will* get out,' said Harry, opening the car door. 'You nearly ran down all those rabbits just now – and I'm sure you ran over a squirrel's tail.'

'Well, your car hasn't a hooter,' said Longbeard. 'So I can't give a warning hoot. I'll buy a hooter when I get to

Brownie Town. It's not very far. Then I shall be able to hoot at anyone in the way.'

He set off without even saying good-bye, and Harry watched him go at top speed down the little curving path. Good gracious! What an adventure! He was glad he wasn't in his car now. Really, Longbeard would have an accident if he wasn't careful!

Harry walked all the way home, and it took him a long time. His mother was out, and there was only Mrs Kelly the cook to talk to. She wouldn't believe a word he said if he told her of his adventure! So he didn't tell anyone.

After tea Harry went out into the garden – and would you believe it, there was his little red and yellow car inside the shed where he always kept it! Yes, there it was, shining as brightly as ever.

Harry ran to it. 'Oh! So Longbeard has brought you back already! I wonder if he caught the thief!'

Then he stopped in surprise. His car had a hooter on the steering-wheel – the finest hooter you ever saw! Harry pressed it. HOOT-TOOT-HOOT! What a noise it made! It frightened two blackbirds off a nearby tree, and made the next-door cat jump off the wall at once!

'He's left me the hooter he said he would buy in Brownie Town!' said Harry in delight. 'And what's this on the seat?'

It was a large bag of sweets. Harry had never before seen sweets like them – they were such queer shapes and colours! Under the bag was a note:

I caught him and spanked him. Here are some of the sweets he stole from me. You'll like them. You can keep the hooter, I don't want it now.

Longbeard.

So that was how Harry got the wonderful hooter on his little car. You should just hear it when he comes at top speed down the lane. Here he is – Hoot-toot-hoot! HOOT-TOOT-HOOT!

The Chocolate Cockerel

Once there was a piece of chocolate in the shape of a cockerel. The chocolate cockerel stood right In the very middle of a sweetshop window, and all the children came to look at him. He was very proud of himself indeed.

'I am the Chocolate Cockerel!' he crowed. 'I am the Chocolate Cockerel! I am the handsomest bird in the world, for I am the Chocolate Cockerel!'

He was priced at two pounds fifty pence, and none of the children that came to look at the cockerel could afford to buy him. They just stood and looked at him.

One day the chocolate cockerel got a dreadful shock. Just next to him stood a little chicken in chocolate, with a

marzipan egg on its back. It had stood by him for quite a long time, and the chocolate cockerel had got quite friendly with it.

The suddenly the hand of the shopkeeper stretched out into the window and the little chick with the egg was lifted out – and, oh my, the next thing that the cockerel saw was the chick in the hand of a little boy outside the window – and the little boy was eating the chick's head off!

That seemed perfectly dreadful to the chocolate cockerel! And then what do you think the little boy said? He said, 'Ha, Chocolate Cockerel! Your turn next! You look so proud, but wait till I eat you! When my uncle gives me some money tomorrow, I'll come and buy you!'

That made the chocolate cockerel shiver and shake. It put him into a temper and a fright both together, and he simply didn't know what to do.

'To think that I, the Chocolate Cockerel, should be eaten by a horrid little boy with dirty hands!' he cried. 'I am the Chocolate Cockerel, the handsomest bird in the world! I will not be eaten!'

'Chocolate is made to be eaten, ' said a marzipan potato. 'Don't be so proud, Chocolate Cockerel. You are meant to be eaten, like the rest of us.'

But the Chocolate Cockerel wouldn't believe it. He made up his mind to run away before the little boy could buy him. Then he would find a farmyard and show all the animals and birds there that he was the finest and handsomest bird in the world!

But he didn't get a chance to run away till the little boy came next day to buy him. Then he gave a loud squawk and jumped out of the window, landed on the shop counter, jumped to the floor, and raced to the door and out of it before the shopkeeper or the surprised little boy could stop him.

'I am the Chocolate Cockerel!' he crowed, as he strutted down the street. 'I am the Chocolate Cockerel! I am the handsomest bird in the world, for I am the Chocolate Cockerel!'

A passing horse snapped at him, for he was fond of chocolate. But the cockerel neatly leapt to one side and strutted on, crowing loudly.

Soon he came to the market and saw all the turkeys, geese and ducks there. They stared at him in surprise, and a fat little hen asked him what he was.

'What am I?' said the chocolate cockerel scornfully. 'Can't you see with your eyes, little hen! I am the Chocolate Cockerel!'

'What use are you?' asked a duck. 'Can you lay eggs?'

'No,' said the cockerel. 'I would scorn to.'

'Do you grow feathers for down

pillows?' asked a goose.

No,' said the cockerel. 'I would scorn to.'

'You don't seem much use!' said all the birds together, and they laughed loudly. That made the chocolate cockerel very angry. He flew to the horse-trough on his chocolate wings and crowed as loudly as he could.

'I am the Chocolate Cockerel!' he crowed. 'I am the Chocolate Cockerel!' I am the handsomest bird in the world, for I am the Chocolate Cockerel!'

A little girl heard him and stared at him in wonder. When she saw that he was made of chocolate, she thought she would like to eat him. So she suddenly put out her hand to take him, and if the chocolate cockerel hadn't been very

quick, he would have been caught. He jumped down just in time, and tore off as fast as he could, dodging between the feet of horses, dogs, sheep and men very cleverly indeed.

I must really find a farmyard, he thought. Then I will get them to make me king, for I am the handsomest bird

in the world – there is no doubt of that. Then I shall be very happy.

So he wandered on till he came to a fine farmyard. There was a pig in it, with eight piglets. There was a donkey looking over a gate. There were two goats tied up near by. There were horses and cows, and so many turkeys, geese, hens and ducks that the chocolate cockerel couldn't have counted them if he had tried.

He flew up on the wall and flapped his wings.

'Listen, all of you!' he cried. 'I am the Chocolate Cockerel! I am the handsomest bird in the world, for I am the Chocolate Cockerel!'

'I am clever!' he cried. 'I am wise. I am the wise and clever Chocolate Cockerel!'

All the animals and birds stared solemnly at him. Rover, the farmyard

dog, licked his lips, and looked longingly at the Chocolate Cockerel.

'I am wiser than any of you. I am a great and wonderful bird, for I am the Chocolate Cockerel!'

'If you are so wise, why do you stand in the sun?' asked Rover.

'Why shouldn't I?' asked the Cockerel angrily. 'You stand in the sun! Why shouldn't I?'

All the farmyard animals and birds turned to stare at him, and the Chocolate Cockerel felt very proud. He crowed more loudly than ever.

'You are chocolate and I am not,' said the dog, and all the animals and birds stared harder than ever; for something was happening to the Chocolate Cockerel!'

His wings dropped, his beak grew longer. His tail began to lose its shape.

He was melting, and he didn't know it. The sun was much too strong for him.

But he wasn't going to get down from the wall, not he.

'I shall stand in the sun as much as I like!' he cried. 'I am the Chocolate Cockerel! I am the Chocolate Cockerel! I am the handsomest bird in – the – world – for – I –'

What was the matter with the Chocolate Cockerel? He could crow no more! He could no longer flap his wings. He had melted in the hot sun! There he lay on the wall, a big pool of brown chocolate. Poor, silly old Chocolate Cockerel!

'Ah, well,' said Rover, the farmyard dog. 'It's a pity to waste anything!'

And he ran up to the wall and licked up all that was left of the vain Chocolate Cockerel!'

Funny-Face

The children had been to a party, and they had brought a funny balloon back with them.

It had a smiling face painted on it, and feathers gummed to the top for hair. It was really very funny.

Jane hung it up on the centre light, twisting the string round it so that the balloon swung to and fro below.

'Funny-Face!' said Jane. 'I wonder what the toys will think of you, grinning away like that!'

They went to bed and left Funny-Face swinging gently to and fro. The toys came out and looked at it.

'Who are you?' said the clown. Funny-Face didn't say a word. It just swung gently to and fro, smiling and

smiling. The feathers on the top quivered as if they were laughing too.

'It's rude to grin like that and never say a word,' said the bear. 'What is your name? We heard the children call you Funny-Face.'

Funny-Face just smiled and said nothing. The clown got very angry.

'Who do you think you are, swinging there above our heads and laughing at us?' he said. 'Come down and tell us your name.'

To his great surprise, Funny-Face swung faster – and then the string slipped from the lamp and the balloon floated gently down to the toys. The wind had blown in at the window that very minute and loosened the string!

The toys were quite scared when they saw Funny-Face so near to them. They ran away. Funny-Face smiled and smiled.

The clown soon felt bold when he saw that Funny-Face didn't chase the toys. He came out from his corner.

'Ho! So you've come down to join us! Well, perhaps you will tell us your name now?'

Funny-Face rolled about a little, and didn't say one word. The clown marched right up to it, and glared.

'I smack people who don't answer me!' he said, and he gave the balloon a big smack. It bounced away and then rolled back again, still smiling.

'I don't like your smile,' said the bold clown. 'Stop smiling! And answer me when I speak to you!'

Funny-Face didn't answer. It rolled a little way away from the clown in the wind that came under the door. The clown went after it.

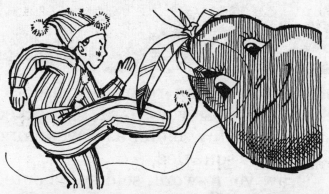

'I shall smack you with *both* my hands and kick you with *both* my feet if you aren't polite enough to say who you are!' he said. And will you believe it, he did just as he said – and, of course, Funny-Face bobbed right away to the

other side of the room, because the clown kicked so very hard. It knocked over a little toy soldier as it went, and the soldier squealed.

'Draw your sword, soldier!' shouted the clown. 'He's getting fierce! How dare he knock you over!'

So the soldier drew his sword – and as the balloon bobbed near him again, he pointed it at Funny-Face, and shouted:

'Any nearer and I will fight you!'

The balloon couldn't help going nearer because the wind under the door blew it again. It bobbed smiling right on to the soldier's sharp sword.

BANG!

What a noise! The toys all fell over, and then sat up again in surprise, looking for Funny-Face.

'He's gone,' said the clown.

'But he's left his feathers behind,' said the soldier.

'And his string,' said the bear. '*Where's* he gone? I can't see him anywhere. Did we frighten him away?'

'He must have flown out of the window,' said the clown. 'But what was that terrible bang?'

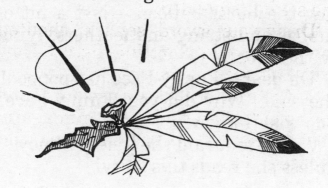

Nobody knew. They were all very scared and they crept into the toy cupboard and were soon fast asleep.

Jane heard the bang and got out of bed. She padded into the playroom, and saw the burst balloon – just a bit of rubber and string and feathers, lying on the floor.

'Oh dear – Funny-Face has popped!' she said. 'Why did you, Funny-Face? I do wish I knew!'

Well, I'm afraid she'll never know – unless she reads this story!

The Ugly Old Scarecrow

Peter and Jane often went for a walk in the fields near their home. There was one walk they liked very much because there were four stiles to climb over, and a little swing-gate to go through.

One day the farmer planted seeds in one of his fields. The birds came and pecked them up, so he put an old scarecrow in the middle of the field to scare them away.

Peter and Jane suddenly saw the scarecrow as they were climbing over the stile to go into the field.

'What's that?' said Jane, frightened.

'A scarecrow,' said Peter. 'I don't like him, do you?'

'No. I can't bear him,' said Jane. 'He frightens me. He's so ugly.'

The Ugly Old Scarecrow

The scarecrow was indeed very ugly. His head was a turnip stuck on a pole. The farmer had cut eyes, nose and mouth out of the turnip head. He had a very old hat on, whose ragged ribbons flapped in the wind. The coat he wore had once belonged to the farmer, and was dirty and ragged, full of holes.

He wore a ragged pair of trousers that flapped wildly whenever the wind blew. His arms were sticks that stuck out straight.

He stared straight at the two children with his turnip eyes. 'I don't like him,' said Jane. 'I know he's not alive, but really he almost looks as if he could walk across the field right up to the stile!'

'Don't be silly,' said Peter. But he didn't like the look of the scarecrow either. The wind blew and the scarecrow's clothes flapped hard, scaring all the rooks away at once.

'Let's go another way,' said Peter, and he climbed back over the stile. 'We won't come this way any more. Do you think we're cowards, Jane?'

'Yes. I suppose we are,' said Jane. 'It's a pity because this is our best walk. It's such fun to go to the farm this way–and it takes ages and ages if we have to go the other way round.'

Still, they didn't think they would walk through the scarecrow's field again, even if it made them feel little cowards! Jane knew she was silly, but she couldn't help feeling that the scarecrow might chase her.

The ugly old scarecrow came into her dreams that night. Jane screamed and Mother came to see what was the matter.

'I dreamt that the scarecrow was running after me,' sobbed Jane. 'I'm

afraid of him.'

'What's the matter with him, poor old scarecrow?' said Mother. 'Out there in the wind and the rain all alone, with no one to say hello–and the children running away from him because they're frightened!'

All the same, whatever her mother said Jane still didn't feel much better. So the very next day Mother went to take a look at the old scarecrow herself. How she laughed when she saw the poor old turnip-head man flapping his clothes at the birds and scaring them away. She saw something else too, and she stood and looked for a long time.

On Saturday she spoke to Peter and Jane. 'I'm going to take you for a walk. Get your things on.'

They put on their hats and coats, and went with their mother. She took them to the field where the scarecrow stood, his hat all crooked on his turnip-head.

'Oh! We don't want to go through this field,' said Jane, in alarm.

'But I want to show you a rabbit's home, and a robin's nest with three eggs in it,' said Mother. The children stared at her in delight.

'A robin's nest–with eggs in! Oh, we haven't seen one this year!' said Peter.

'Show me,' said Jane, and took hold of her mother's hand very tightly. She went over the stile and the two children followed.

Mother didn't follow the path round the edge of the field. She walked carefully over the field itself, right up to the scarecrow! The two children hung behind, not liking this at all.

Still, their mother was with them, so nothing horrid could happen. They followed her slowly.

'You said you'd show us a robin's nest and a rabbit's home,' said Peter. 'I can't see either of them.'

'No, the dear old scarecrow is guarding them well,' said Mother. 'He's keeping them safe. He scares the rooks, but he likes the rabbits and the robins. Scarecrow, where do the little rabbits live?'

The scarecrow stared at Mother, and then one of his trouser-legs moved in the wind. Below it they saw a rabbit-hole and Jane felt sure she could see a pair of ears ready to pop out as soon as they were gone!

'Oh! This is where the rabbits live!' she
cried. 'Where is the robin's nest,

old scarecrow?'

The scarecrow looked at them all, and Jane saw that his face wasn't really ugly, only weird, because it was made of turnip. He swung his coat in the wind, and Peter gave a cry of delight.

'Look! The nest is in his pocket! And there are three speckled eggs there. Mummy, isn't that wonderful, a nest in a scarecrow's pocket?'

'Yes,' said Mother. 'He must be glad that the bright-eyed robin likes him enough to build in his pocket, and that the rabbits trust him enough to make a hole by his feet so that they can pop in and out. It's a pity that children are afraid of him, isn't it?'

'I'm as brave as a robin any day!' said Peter, and he actually patted the scarecrow on the shoulder. 'Scarecrow, we aren't afraid of you any more! If you are the robin's friend and the rabbit's, you're ours, too! We'll come and see you every day.'

And they do. The old scarecrow must be very pleased!